WEEKLY READER CHILDREN'S BOOK CLUB PRESENTS

Anatole
and the Toyshop

ANATOLE
and the Toyshop

by EVE TITUS

pictures by
PAUL GALDONE

McGRAW-HILL BOOK COMPANY
New York • St. Louis • San Francisco •
Dusseldorf • London • Mexico • Panama •
Sydney • Toronto

FONDLY, FOR MY SON RICK

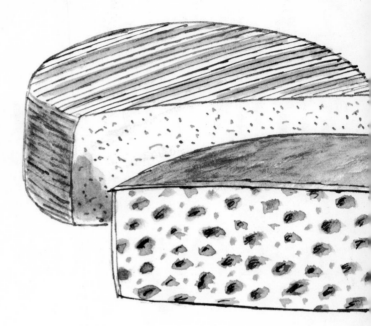

Library of Congress Catalog Card Number: 70-110962

Weekly Reader Children's Book Club Edition
Primary Division

ISBN 07-064885-9
2345678 HDEC 7654321

MEMBER OF THE AUTHORS LEAGUE OF AMERICA

In all France there was no mouse more beloved than Anatole.
He was the happy husband of his dear wife Doucette
and the proud *Papa* of their six charming children.

Most mice lived on people's leftovers, but not Anatole.
He earned his family's food by working as Cheese Taster
at the Duval Factory, so late at night that nobody saw him.
Everyone, even M'sieu Duval, thought that Anatole was a man.

Joy in his work, joy at home—could any mouse wish for more?
But it all ended on the dreadful day his family disappeared!

Arrived home that morning, after a long night's work,
Anatole found a note from Doucette in the typewriter.

Dear Anatole,

Your cheese is on the table.
There's no school today, so
we're off to see the sights
of Paris. Don't be lonely—
we'll be back by afternoon.

Your loving wife,
Doucette

P.S. Love from your children

PAUL AND PAULETTE
CLAUDE AND CLAUDETTE
GEORGES AND GEORGETTE
x x x x x

Anatole passed the day pleasantly in the mouse village,
then sat waiting for his family to come home.
The sun set, the moon rose, and darkness descended.
Far into the night he waited, but nobody came.

He went upstairs, his mind filled with a million fears—
cats and mousetraps and all sorts of terrible things!

When his good friend Gaston came by, Anatole asked a favor.
"I'm too upset to work tonight. Please go in my place."

After Gaston had gone to the cheese factory,
Anatole made himself fall asleep,
but he had such frightening dreams about his dear ones
that he made himself wake up.

Sadly he stood at the window,
watching and waiting and worrying,
wondering what might have happened. . . .

After riding around Paris, his family had started for home.
Feeling tired, they sat down to rest outside a big toyshop,
but no sooner did they sit down than they fell fast asleep.

Just then M'sieu Barat, the toyshop owner, spied the mice.
(Behind his back the neighbors called this man *Bad Barat*.
He never gave toys to the poor at Christmas, and had once said,
"If they can't buy toys, let them make their own!")

Now this sly man smiled and said, "Just what I need!
With mice riding in my front window, business will boom!"

And scooping up the sleeping mice in a butterfly net,
he carefully carried them inside, bicycles and all.

The way into the window was through huge glass doors
that went from floor to ceiling—Barat opened these doors.

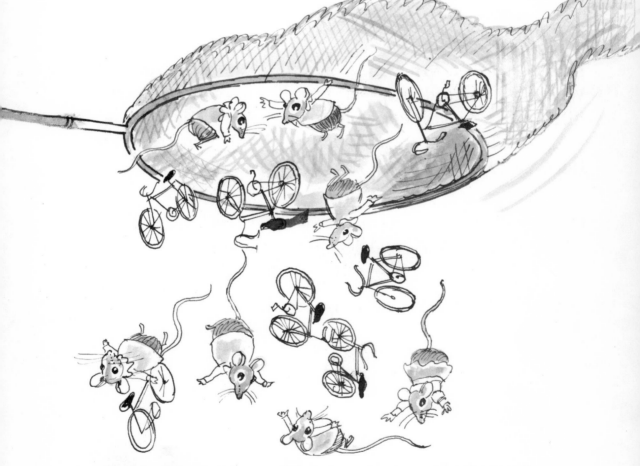

Shaking the net, he tumbled the mice into the window!
Then he closed the big glass doors and latched them tight.

13

The mice awoke to find themselves in a make-believe park,
with cleverly made flowers and grass and trees and bridges.
Tiny dolls sat on benches, toy soldiers stood at attention,
and all around the park went winding pathways.

The children thought it pretty, but Doucette shook her head.
"Pretty or not, it's nothing but a prison! Ssh! Listen—"

They heard a scratching at the glass doors, and turned around.
"HORRORS!" cried Doucette. "IT'S A BIG FAT WHITE CAT!"

Bad Barat picked up the cat, saying, "Calm yourself, Clotilde!
When these mice ride in my window, all Paris will come to stare,
I'll sell toys morning, noon, and night! And after closing-time,
you, Clotilde, will be my watchdog—or should I say *watchcat?*
If they try to gnaw through the floor, fetch me at once."

Opening the glass door a crack, he pointed a stick at the mice.
"Ride!" he commanded. "All but the mother—RIDE!"

"Obey him," said Doucette softly, "or he'll let the cat at us!"

14

So the mice mounted their bicycles, and the crowds came quickly,
delighted at the sight of the wee riders in the window.
Many people stepped inside to buy toys, and Barat rejoiced,
for the pile of francs in his money-drawer grew higher and higher!

Riding was fun at first, but when the mice stopped to rest,
Barat's stick rapped at the glass to make them keep going.
Fearing the cat, they rode 'round and 'round and 'round,
'til their little legs could scarcely turn the pedals,
'til their tired paws could hardly hold the handlebars.

Then some ladies told Barat that the mice must rest, and he agreed,
afraid he'd be reported to the police for cruelty to animals.
To make sure the mice wouldn't be too weak to ride in the evening,
he threw them tiny snips of cheese, almost too tiny to see.

My poor darlings, thought Doucette—if only Anatole would come!

Nine o'clock was closing-time, and Barat sent the people home.
Putting Clotilde on a little table near the window, he said,
"Sleep well, sweet mice—I'm leaving a watchcat to watch you!"

Then he dimmed the lights and went to bed.

Clotilde's green eyes gleamed. "Stupid little mice!
Shall I tell you a secret my master told me? Hmmm?
When the people of Paris grow weary of watching you,
Clotilde shall have a special treat—*a mouse a day!*"

"*Monstre!*" screamed Doucette, holding her children close.

Then, to them, "Fear not! Your Papa will soon save us!"

But in her heart she wondered—does Anatole know where we are?

At that moment there came a tap-tap-tapping at Anatole's window.
It was Pierre the Pigeon, bringing his friend the bad news.
"Alas, your wife and children are prisoners in a toyshop window!"

Then he told all about Bad Barat and Clotilde the Cat.

"That cruel man!" cried Anatole. "Please, Pierre, fly me there!"

Perched on Pierre's back, Anatole stared at the night sky,
his brain busy with plans for saving his loved ones.

Thought he—there must be mouse tunnels under the toyshop floor.
If my family can't gnaw *down* through the floor, because of the cat,
then why can't carpenter mice saw *up* through the floor?
The sawed wood will drop into the tunnel, leaving an opening above.
My family will jump down, and away we'll go! But what of the cat?

Just then Pierre glided to the ground in front of the toyshop.

Doucette was weeping, the children were sleeping.
She pressed her face against the glass. "Save us, Anatole!
Poor children—the cheese they get wouldn't feed a flea!
They ride, ride, ride, from morn 'til noon 'til night,
and after closing-time, that watchcat never stops watching us!"

Anatole glared at Clotilde, who glared back, as if to say,
"I'm too smart to let them escape. Give up and go home!"
But Anatole winked at Doucette, and declared,
"This I shall prove—*cats may be clever, but mice are more so!*"

Softly, so the cat could not hear, he told his plan, then said,
"We'll arrive very late tomorrow night, after Barat goes to bed.
But who'll keep the watchcat from watching? Who'll trick the cat?"
Doucette dried her tears. "Me, myself, and I! What shall I do?"

"Anything! Make funny faces, do silly dances, wiggle your ears!
Keep Clotilde's eyes on *you* when the children jump, then follow!
I'll be waiting below in the tunnel to catch all of you.
How furious the cat will be when she sees she's been tricked!
She'll run to Barat, he'll run to the window, but—NO MICE!"

Doucette blew him a kiss. "Genius! 'Til tomorrow night, *chéri.*"

All the way home Anatole did arithmetic in his head—
if seven mice with seven saws sawed for seven minutes—
if ten mice with ten saws—if forty mice with forty saws—

Just as they reached the mouse village,
he decided upon four mice with four saws,
because they wouldn't get in one another's way.
Pleased with his plan, he thanked Pierre and went to bed.

Late the next night Anatole and four carpenter mice entered a secret tunnel under the toyshop window. Chalking a square on the ceiling, he paced to and fro while the carpenters sawed swiftly and steadily away.

When Gaston arrived, Anatole said, "The work goes well, but for some strange reason, I'm as nervous as a cat! Will my plan fail? I'd better see what's what with Barat!"

Ordering the mice to stop work, he raced outside with Gaston.

The hour was midnight, but the shop was still open,
brightly lit and filled with people!

A big sign on the door told the mice the reason:

PEOPLE OF PARIS!
THE MICE IN MY WINDOW ARE
SO POPULAR THAT FROM NOW ON
MY TOYSHOP WILL STAY OPEN
ALL DAY AND ALL NIGHT.
(signed) Bruno Barat

P.S. Don't forget to buy toys!

Anatole said sadly, "Alas for the plans of mice and men!
Escape is impossible, with all those crowds at the window.
They'd surely see the saws come through, and so would Barat.
He'd scoop my family up in his net, then cover the opening."
The two mice stood silent, in deepest despair,
and suddenly two wild-eyed alleycats sprang at them!

The mice ran for their lives, into a mousehole near a petshop.
And while the alleycats howled outside, Anatole made a new plan,
one so dreadfully dangerous that at first he felt afraid.
He told his idea to Gaston, who cried, *"Non, non, non!*
I beg you not to risk your life! Think of another plan!"*

But Anatole had made up his mind. "This plan is the best.
I must save my family, regardless of the risk to myself!"

When the angry cats had gone, the mice entered the petshop,
and helped themselves to all the catnip they could carry.
"Gaston, go and collect the carpenters' cheese," said Anatole,
"and put it in the petshop to pay for the catnip.
Cats often eat mice, but catnip is a rare and special treat.
Too bad they don't have it more often—they love it madly!"

Outside, Anatole loaded the catnip on his bicycle, and rode off.

"Good luck on your misson!" called Gaston. "You'll need it!"

And what was this hero's mission? Believe it or not—
to lure the cats of Paris to the toyshop of Barat!

From all over Paris came the cats,
to follow the mouse with the catnip!
He scattered the stuff behind him,
and it didn't matter that he was a mouse—
all they could see and sniff was catnip!

Onward they ran, eyes glued to the ground!
Cats of all colors, cats of all kinds—
green-eyed, blue-eyed, two-eyed, *one*-eyed,
long-tailed, short-tailed, *no*-tailed,
tomcats, tabby cats, kitten cats,
plump and pretty, sleek and shiny,
skinny, scrawny, tawny, tiny!

Onward they charged, that army of cats—
from fences, from rooftops, from doorways,
from attics, from alleys, from hallways,
from gutters, from garbage-cans, from gateways!

And Anatole, rememb'ring a poem he knew,
The Charge of the Light Brigade, cried,
"Voilà! The Charge of the Cat Brigade!
There are cats to the right of me,
cats to the left of me, cats in back of me!
Onward, Mouse! The time has come
to lead them into the toyshop!"

A N D   H E   D I D ! ! !

Naturally, Anatole was followed—by sixty-six excited cats!
Scattering the last of the catnip, he stood on top of a toy train
to see what would happen.

The shop, still jammed and crammed with people,
was now jammed and crammed with people and cats!
Arms and legs and paws and claws were in a terrible tangle!

Ladies were screaming and squealing and squirming—
men were shouting and scowling and struggling—
cats were screeching and scratching and spitting!

Then all the people made a mad dash for the door—
the uproar could be heard at the top of the Eiffel Tower!
OUCH! OW! MEOW! MEOW! OUCH! OW! MEOW! MEOW!

31

A few people fell, and got catnip on their clothes.
Cats climbed all over them, gobbling up the catnip.

Anatole shrugged his shoulders and said, *"C'est la vie.*
I'm not too sorry about the people—did even *one* of them
tell the police about the prisoners in the window?"

Then, knowing that cats on a catnip spree do crazy things,
he watched them act like foolish clowns.

Some cats spun 'round and 'round, noses in the air.
Some tried to stand on their heads, but kept tumbling down.
Some wept and wailed and howled and yowled for more catnip.
And Clotilde and a frisky friend were dancing on their toes!
Flat on the floor was Barat, and ten cats sat on his chest,
scrapping and snarling and squabbling for the catnip in his clothes!

In all the hullabaloo, who'd notice a mere midget of a mouse?
Nobody! Anatole wheeled his bicycle to the door,
waved farewell to the topsy-turvy toyshop, and took his leave.

33

Darting into the tunnel, he told the carpenters to work fast.
Swiftly they sawed away, then stepped nimbly aside
as a square of wood dropped down, leaving an opening above.

"Pass the bicycles to me," called Anatole, and this was done.
Then, one by one the children jumped, and their mother followed,
each to be caught and kissed and hugged by Anatole.

Moonlight brightened their joyful journey home.

At the mouse village, all were awake to welcome them.
Hearing of the Charge of the Cat Brigade, the Mayor said,
"This master mind should take my place—I resign!"
And as Anatole accepted the great honor, the crowd roared,
"VIVE ANATOLE, THE MAYOR MAGNIFIQUE!"

And Bad Barat? Poor man! After the Night of the Cats,
just *seeing* one made him shiver and shake and quiver and quake!
So he sold his shop, sold his cat, and moved far away.

Told of this, Doucette declared, "Good riddance to bad rubbish!"

And what do you think was Anatole's *real* reward—
being the most honored mouse in all France?

Non! Having his dear ones home again was his real reward.

For if you asked him, he would say,
"Mayors are important, but families are more so.
Always my family comes first in my heart!"

F I N I S

Date Due

8-21			
8-26			
Nov 8			